HEARTSTONES

Ruth Rendell's first novel, *From Doon with Death*, appeared in 1964, and since then her reputation and readership have grown steadily with each new book. She has now received eight ̶ ̶ ̶ ̶ ̶ r awards for her work: thre̶ ̶ ̶ Mystery Writers ̶ ̶ ̶ ̶ Gold Dagg̶ ̶ ̶ for *A Dem̶ ̶ ̶ National B̶ ̶ for *Lake of ̶ ̶ Dagger Awa̶ ̶ ̶ ̶ ̶ ̶ ̶ ̶ ̶ ̶ ne novel for *The Tree of ̶ ̶ ̶ ̶ ̶ Crime Writers' Gold Dagger Award for 1986's best crime novel for *Live Flesh*, and in 1987 the Crime Writers' Gold Dagger Award for *A Fatal Inversion*, written under the name Barbara Vine. Her books have been translated into fifteen languages and are also published to great acclaim in the United States. Ruth Rendell is married and lives in a sixteenth-century farmhouse in Suffolk

A R E N A
N O V E L L A

ALSO AVAILABLE BY RUTH RENDELL

HEARTSTONES
Ruth Rendell

ARENA
NOVELLA

An Arena book
Published by Arrow Books Limited
Brookmount House, 62–65 Chandos Place, London WC2N 4NW

An imprint of Century Hutchinson Limited

London Melbourne Sydney Auckland Johannesburg
and agencies throughout the world

Originally published in the Hutchinson Novella series

General Editor: Frank Delaney

First published by Hutchinson 1987

Arena edition 1988

© Text Kingsmarkham Enterprises 1987

Typeset in Monophoto Photina by
Vision Typesetting, Manchester

Printed and bound in Great Britain by
The Guernsey Press Co. Ltd,
Guernsey, C. I.

ISBN 0 09 953490 8

HEARTSTONES

In those days I had never given a thought to poisoning and I can be sure of this, that I had nothing to do with our mother's death. I was even upset by it, though not as upset as Spinny who cried and sobbed. It was our grandmother who told us she was dead. We must have looked like one of those Victorian paintings that tell a story, 'The Long Engagement' or 'The Awakening of Conscience', only ours would have been called 'Poor Motherless Children', Grandmother with Spinny on her lap and her arm about me, drawing my head against her shoulder, whispering to us what had happened.

Though I had nothing to do with it, it was no surprise to me. I knew she would die from the moment I overheard her telling Luke she would not have the operation, she would rather die than be mutilated. Instead she went to a naturopath who made her eat nothing but raw vegetables. Luke said the word alone was enough for him, 'naturopath', a bastard hybrid of Latin and Greek. I knew the cancer would not mind raw vegetables, would be scornful of them even, as an animal despises a trap set with unalluring bait.

Spinny had had little warning. She thought our mother would get better and come home, so she cried from shock as well as grief. I rested my head against my grandmother's shoulder, smelling the Yardley Freesia with which her twinsets are impregnated, wondering why Luke had not come to tell us himself. He was still at the hospital; he had phoned his mother, but I would rather have waited, I would rather he had told us himself. The phone rang again and for a minute or two Grandmother left us alone.

'I want to see Luke,' I said to Spinny. 'I want to see how he has taken it.'

Still crying, Spinny said, 'He will be broken-hearted.'

She picks up these expressions from the women who come to clean our house and cook for us.

'He won't be,' I said. 'He has me.' Feeling tender towards her because she has lost her mother, I corrected that. 'He has us.'

'It's not like a wife, Rosemary says.'

Rosemary is one of the women, gossipy, given to inane chat, a mine of clichés, Luke says, which made me see a deep cave and men on their knees with picks and hammers, mining clichés out from between the strata: here's another, 'He broke his heart,' and another, 'It was a merciful release!'

'It's better than a wife, Spinny,' I said. 'We're half made out of him.'

Despina is her name really but everyone calls her Spinny. Mine is Elvira and no one has ever called me Elly. Our mother was devoted to the operas of Mozart and Luke used to say that if she had ever had a son she would have wanted to call him Figaro. We all have unusual names, except my mother whose name was Anne. Perhaps that was why we didn't like it and always called her Mother while it never seemed to have occurred to us – to me, rather, for Spinny of course was guided by me – to call our father anything but Luke.

'He will be here in half an hour,' Grandmother said.
We were in her house. We had been staying there for
the past two days. I longed for home. I thought how it
would have been if I could have watched for Luke from
our drawing room window, opened the door to him with
grave dignity, led him to his study and there sat close to
him in silence. But to my grandmother I was a child still,
though in fact I had never been one, was born old, and
this Luke knows. He knows it privately, secretly, it is one
of our secrets. When he first began to tell me stories from
the Greek I thought that I too was like Athene and had
sprung fully-armed from my father's head. I can still
remember the shock of learning that I came instead from
my mother's womb: a damp dark place, a warm well
lined with weed and limpets and sea anemones was how
I saw it, whereas the matrix from which I would have
chosen to spring was a gilded dome like a temple, Luke's
head that housed Luke's mind.

I refused to eat Grandmother's tea. She usually
expected people to drop down dead if they did not eat
something at least every two hours but this time she
understood or thought she understood. She took my
hand under the cloth and squeezed it. She is a sweet
woman, my grandmother, and you can see Luke is her
son, for she too is tall and fair and symmetrical and as if
carved from marble. Luke and she and I are all like that,
but Spinny is her mother's child, plump, dark, ox-eyed.

Spinny ate. For comfort, Grandmother said, plying her
with Viennese Whirls. Eating means very little to me and
I would forget to do it unless there were someone there to
remind me. The body I find boring compared with the
soul, which is surely the most interesting thing in this

world. So I did not eat but sat there wondering if Luke would take us home and I thought I would ask him to, though it is not my way to plead. I waited for him at the oval mahogany table with its fine lawn cloth that has a border of drawn thread work, seeing my face reflected in the silver teapot, Grandmother's hands busy with the Flora Danica porcelain, hands that had been beautiful but are now distorted by arthritis – oh, the body, the damned body! – Spinny's little round face on which a tear had dried and left a drift of salt like a petal.

Luke had a key and let himself in quietly. He and I and Grandmother are quiet deft movers, gliding silently. I did not speak. I gazed intently at him, looking for those signs the cliché women said would be there, the drawn look, the hollow eye, the trembling lip. There was nothing. His wonderful looks were unimpaired, the light tan on his skin, the unclouded blue eyes, the expression that is at the same time ardent, eager, spiritual, and which belongs exclusively to those of super-normal intellect. In that moment I became all fire and air, I had no flesh, I wanted nothing from him but to see him, be in the same room with him, fuse our souls.

He kissed his mother, laid his hands on little Spinny's shoulders and kissed her forehead. But when she broke once more into tears he was unable to comfort her and leaving her to Grandmother, turned his eyes on me. He did not touch me, we hardly ever touched, but we were in total silent communion.

'Shall we go home now, Elvira?' he said.

The house we live in is in the centre of the city – near, though not in, the cathedral close. Luke, principally a teacher at the university, is also in holy orders and his

10

father was Dean here. Our house is very old, in part fifteenth-century, and very elegant with none of that exposed beam and studwork Luke says is vulgar. It is also reputed to be haunted. There are various ghosts, audible rather than visible; a woman who walks the passages, her heels tap-tapping on boards of wood though our floors are carpeted, a voice that whispers one's name, a cat that *is* visible. I have never seen or heard of any of these and nor has Luke. Mother claimed to have seen the cat once but why she should have thought it a ghost I don't know. Surely a cat is far more likely to be a real cat? She used to do a little writing for a local magazine and wanted to do a piece on our ghosts but Luke read to her this passage from Fielding:

'The only supernatural agents which can in any manner be allowed to us moderns are ghosts but of these I would advise an author to be extremely sparing. They are indeed like arsenic and other dangerous drugs in physic, to be used with the utmost caution. Nor would I advise them at all in those works or by those authors to which or to whom a horse laugh in the reader would be any great prejudice or mortification.'

He always has the apt commentary, the *mot juste*.

Spinny began to hear and see the ghosts after Mother died. It was probably a way of attracting attention to herself. I fancy she felt Luke and I had become all in all to each other while she was a little out in the cold. I got her to help me answer the multitude of letters that came to us, condoling with us in our loss. It seemed to me that people would be touched to receive a reply in her rounded childish hand, her real expressions of grief untouched by sophistication.

'I saw the cat last night, Elvira,' she said to me, sealing

11

up the envelope to Mrs Fitzboyne, wife of the Rural Dean. We were working at the desk in the drawing room, its long mullioned window giving on to Lady Lane where fallen lime flowers lay. 'I saw the cat come into my bedroom. It came in through the window and sat on my bookcase.'

'You had better keep your window shut in future,' I said smiling at her.

'When I shut the window it comes through the panel in the door.'

So I spoke to Luke about her. Sometimes it falls to his lot to preach and he was in his study writing a sermon. The subject, I believe, was spiritual wickedness in high places. I love his study. It is my favourite corner of this whole house, for it is full of Luke, his books, his papers, great tomes and encyclopaedias and theological works, but all kept exquisitely tidy. It would never occur to Luke to take the attitude of some learned men and forbid a cleaner to enter his study. What harm could Rosemary or Sheila do here where every book is behind glass, every sheet of paper neatly stacked, every note the topmost sheet of a pad, the pen he used laid at a perfect right angle across it? On the window-sill was a copper bowl of narcissi, snow-white ones of course, arranged there by me before I went to school that morning, but Luke has taken one from the arrangement and laid it on the polished oak of his desk, very near to his left hand so that he might sometimes touch its cold white skin while he wrote.

'It is always before she goes to sleep,' I said. 'A kind of waking dream, I suppose.'

'What should we do, Elvira?' he asked me.

'If you could sit with her until she goes to sleep. I would do it, of course, but it would hardly be the same. She misses Mother. If you would sit with her and hold her hand I am sure she would sleep and after a week or two all these so-called ghosts would be forgotten.'

He looked at me with such tenderness, such profound understanding, as he agreed to help poor little Spinny in this way. Did he know how much it cost me to ask this of him, what a sacrifice I was making for my sister's sake? Of course he did. I will not say my father followed everything that passed in my mind, but he followed everything I wanted him to follow. As soon as I opened the door of the room where my thoughts lived and bred and multiplied he could perceive their movements – only, though, when I opened that door. He knew that the greatest happiness I could enjoy would be in his exclusive society without intruders, and knew too that it was a measure of the maturity his care had fostered in me that I would share him with my little sister.

For this was something I had not always had to do. Spinny had been so much more her mother's child. I was three when she was born and remember with perfect clarity being told I was to have a little brother or sister to play with. This was the way my mother put it to me and I believed her, as what child would not?

The reality is a baby the older sibling is forbidden to touch, for how would that elder one choose to 'play' with the interloper, the thief of a parent's love? By beating it to death, by stamping on its face, by taking the feeble wriggling body to the river and watching the current carry it away downstream. Those are the games to play with a new brother or sister – if the opportunity is given.

I was not given it. Luke was always an attentive father.

'You won't find a man getting up in the night when they cry,' is what Rosemary says. 'That's a woman's job and no amount of this equality is going to change it.'

But Luke got up to me. I cannot remember that I ever wore napkins, that I was once incontinent, but I have been told I was and that Luke came to change my clothes. My mother told me this and – do you know? – I began to love her less afterwards, from the time she told me, laughing, that I was like other babies and wetted and soiled myself. Luke has never alluded to it, only saying that it was as often as not he who comforted me and held me and nursed me when I cried. This I can remember from before I could talk. And when Spinny was born and my mother's whole attention was given to her Luke came to me every time I awoke in the night, every time I called out. I became his child and Spinny our mother's. So it has always been until now when he must try to find room in his heart for her as well.

He did as I asked and sat nightly with her, held her hand. Once or twice I crept in to look at them. There was a light on in the passage but Luke sat in the dark. The glow from outside illuminated his fair hair, his profile, the straight line of his back and the angle of the outstretched arm, the fine tapering slender hand that loosely held Spinny's plump one, so that he looked as if made from bronze and I recalled the statues by Bernini we had seen in Rome. I saw Spinny's eyes open, the lashes quivering, her head slightly turned towards Mother's photograph that stands on her bedside cabinet.

I tiptoed away, soon passing from that lighted passage

into darker parts of the house, walking through the rooms as I often do in the evenings, listening, watching, looking through the windows into the Close or up at the towering walls of the cathedral, floodlit for Easter. Sometimes I listen for the voice that whispers but I hear nothing. Our house is always silent, for none of us cares for music. Luke discouraged my mother's fondness for Mozart and was relieved when her record player was broken. He has forbidden radios to Rosemary and Sheila and if we ever have to employ a builder it is written into the contract that the men bring no transistors with them. These solid old houses exclude sound and our neighbours are never audible.

I looked down on to the cobblestones that we in these parts call 'hearts' because they are said to be the size and shape of human hearts, stones that came centuries ago from the beach at Newhaven, and saw the shadow of a cat crossing them before I saw the cat itself. It was the blue and yellow cat, those colours closely mingled in its coat, that belongs to Mrs Cyprian, the wife of one of our canons. Was it this cat that Spinny had seen coming in through her window?

That was the night I stood by the window speculating about heaven and hell. Surely as good an answer as any is that what is heaven for one species must be hell for another. I imagined a heaven for mice that was a granary filled with never-diminishing piles of varied grains where they might eat in perfect peace all day, but which was also a hell for cats who were confined in tiny cages around the granary walls without food or water or hope of escape, condemned for ever to watch the mice and be watched, gleefully, by them. So might some people's dream of heaven, a place to eat and drink in, to loll in front of television, to play endless records on unbreakable record players, to embrace lovers and be embraced by them, be hell to Luke and me, obliged for all eternity to watch and listen.

He came and stood beside me. These disturbing thoughts vanished and I was enveloped in peace, filled with trust.

'I think we should go away somewhere,' he said. 'For a holiday.'

'Oh, yes,' I said. 'Do let's.'

'Before our terms start.'

It would be the first time he and I had ever been away alone together. Florence, I thought, that was where I should like to go, or one of those smaller, less-frequented Italian cities, Verona, Urbino. Luke and I would walk along the Arno (or the Adige) looking at distant cupolas and càmpaniles, treading each day the marble staircases of picture galleries, silent under the vaults of basilicas. People would take us for brother and sister, a young girl and her older brother, an idea which strangely pleased me.

But I was old for my age, mature, responsible, wise. I was not a child, thinking I could have what I wanted just because I wanted it and at the cost of another's unhappiness.

'We shall have to take Spinny,' I said.

It was too dark to see his face. I was a head shorter than he was then and always had to look up to him. I did look up, for I felt he had sharply turned his head towards me and perhaps made some sound – a sound of distress? Of impatience? I read his thoughts.

'I know, Luke, but we really have no choice.'

'Naturally we shall take Spinny,' he said. 'By "we" I meant you and me and Spinny.

I smiled at him in the dark. What does it matter if the voice, which is a bodily function, an emanation of the body, lies? The soul cannot lie. I left the window silently and he followed me. For an hour or so we would sit and read in his study and then I would go away to bed. Never would Luke tell me it was time for bed; that was not his way with me, for he knew he could rely absolutely on my good sense and that I would invariably leave him and go upstairs at nine-thirty. I sat in one corner of the leather settee, Luke in the other. Of what I was reading I have no precise recollection, Sheridan Lefanu perhaps, or *The Monk* or Horace Walpole. Luke read Newman's *Apologia Pro Vita Sua*, probably for the twentieth time. It was the book he read for solace when anxious or unhappy but also because he liked it and had a special feeling of compassion and admiration for Cardinal Newman, which must have been his reason that night, for he had nothing to be anxious or unhappy about.

The summer passed and with it my sixteenth birthday. We went to Verona and later on, in August, to France; when we came back Luke had set upon Mother's grave in the precincts of the cathedral a headstone of granite, on which was engraved the following epitaph: *Anne, beloved wife of Luke Zoffany, mother of Elvira and Despina*, with her dates and an appropriate text from the Apocrypha.

Spinny started at my school that autumn term. Grandmother took us out to buy her school uniform, though this was something I could have seen to perfectly

well on my own. Not that shopping for clothes gives me
any pleasure. Clothes bore me and I have never been able
to see the need for more than something to wear for
everyday, something for best and various coats to keep
out the cold and the wet. Adorning the body must be one
of mankind's most pathetic and humiliating weaknesses.

Did I say we had no mirrors in our house? This is not
absolutely true as there is a small mirror in the
bathroom, three mirrors in a triptych arrangement on
my mother's dressing table, and I believe Spinny has a
hand mirror with a silver back that Grandmother gave
her. But this is all; not many for a house on four floors
that contains six bedrooms.

I do not want to see my face looking back at me every
day, though I have been told too often that it is a
beautiful face. If it is (as I have also often been told) a
facsimile of Luke's it must be beautiful. My hair I can see
without looking in a glass, for it hangs to below my waist
and has never been cut, never, except when I snip the
ends off myself with Mother's little sewing scissors. But
that day, shopping for Spinny's skirt and blazer, I could
not help catching glimpses of myself in those full-length
mirrors they have in big stores at every turn. I paused
(while Grandmother and Spinny and the assistant
argued about lengths and hems and durability and so
on) and looked critically at my reflection in one of those
mirrors, assessing this structure in which my soul had
made its dwelling place. I had grown. The top of my
head, which had been as high as Luke's heart, now must
reach to his eyebrows. This I knew already, but my
extreme attenuation was new to me. I had almost
reached the degree of thinness I desired, so that I was a

reed-like creature, very nearly transparent and composed, it seemed to me, more of a mysterious alchemy of pearl and mist and silk than flesh and blood. Blood – how I hate the substance and the word! My desire is to reach a point where if I prick myself no blood comes, nothing issues but perhaps a clear ichor, like dew.

'Now that is behind us,' said Grandmother, 'we'll go somewhere nice and have tea. You choose Spinny. Where would you like to go?'

Spinny, of course, chose Carey's Cakeshop in the square where they have cream pastries and genuine Viennese *Sachertorte*. She was not yet thirteen but she weighed more than I.

I drank some tea with lemon and ate a small plain biscuit.

'I had an enormous lunch,' I said.

It was my voice only, my body only, that lied. Spinny was looking at me but she said nothing.

'Your father was very thin at your age,' said Grandmother, 'and you take after him. He had a big appetite too. He would eat a horse, your grandfather used to say, and then look around for the rider.'

Spinny laughed. I wonder that people are amused at the notion of cannibalism but they usually are. The joke that is sure to succeed is some variation on the theme of the poor missionary boiled in the pot. And now I will write down something about me, something that no one knows. I have not come to the menarche. (This is the way I prefer to put it. Other terms I find repellant.) Once or twice before Mother died, this sign of the ability to breed did occur, bringing with it all the attendant horror, blood and filth and smell and pain.... But I cannot write of it. Once Mother was dead the control of it was in my own hands, within my own will. I found I could ensure it never happened again, I could starve it out and see there was no blood to spare. And who would know? Who would ask? Not Luke, never Luke, who is so scarcely of flesh and blood himself; all spirit, compounded of air and fire, his long white hands the fleshless implements of an El Greco portrait, his skin like parchment, his lips as pale as the white rose from my arrangement I found days later on his desk, dead in the bud.

Have I given the impression we lived in isolation, Luke, Spinny and I, in our house on the 'hearts' of Lady Lane? The three of us always alone, making contact only with my grandmother and attended upon by our two handmaids? Of course it was not so. We had friends. Luke had friends at the university and in the church. In Mother's time they had given dinner parties, invited people for drinks, gone to parties, to the theatre in London and the theatre at Chichester, led what is called a social life. With my mother's death this ended for a while. I confess that our quietness, our comparative solitude, suited me better: Luke and I side by side, I reading Greek with him, sitting in on Spinny's Latin lessons – it was of paramount importance in his eyes to give us both that grounding in the classics we could never hope to receive at school – discussing with him some question of theology or philosophy and meekly receiving his corrections or even admonitions, submitting to him my English or history essay for his acute eye, more sensitive and appraising than any teacher's. All this meant more to me than any going out into the world could do, or the gathering of guests under our own roof. Spinny was different, though. Spinny would bring her friends home and Rosemary would take delight in providing them with a 'tea', cheese on toast and fish paste sandwiches and Madeira cake. In her eyes it seemed to make us a more normal household.

'Poor lamb,' she would say, casting up her cow's eyes, twisting the corners of her mouth. 'Poor lamb, having to do that Latin stuff with her dad in the evenings when she's been studying all day. I call it a wicked shame.'

'How interesting,' I said, 'for I call it a privilege.'

'Sarcasm is the lowest form of wit,' she droned.

I, of course, asked her what she thought the highest would be but any answer to that was beyond her.

Luke, naturally, had always spent a good deal of time away from home, principally at the university, staying late or going back there in the evenings. Most of this stopped when Mother died but about a year afterwards it began again. I accepted it without question, though I suffered. We had begun reading *Antigone* together but rather than sit alone over Sophocles in the study, I gave Spinny her Latin lessons myself or idled the time away dreaming of the future. I had very clear plans for it. A career or profession for myself I was not envisaging. Of course I should go to university but to the one here rather than to Oxford or Cambridge, for I have never been away from home except to my grandmother's and on holidays. I have never, but for those few days before my mother's death, slept under a different roof from Luke's. I can see no reason why I ever should. I saw myself as an eternal student, working for more degrees, for a doctorate, and always sharing this house with Luke. The book entitled 'Noogenesis' that Luke means to write we should work on together, it would be the greatest theological work of the century. Spinny, of course, would marry. At thirteen she already has a boy friend. A boy with spots and an Adam's Apple that sticks out of his throat like a spike, sometimes walks her home from school and takes her to play table tennis at the youth club.

Many evenings I have sat alone, thinking of these things and listening (out of pure academic curiosity) for the footsteps that make a clacking noise though they walk on carpet, for the voice that whispers. One evening, the only one he spent at home in that whole week, Luke told Spinny and me the story that is the origin of the cat ghost. He had known of it for years, he said, having unearthed his information from some ancient archives, but had never related it to us for fear of adding to Spinny's troubles. But it was a while now since she had seen the cat.

'You may not know this,' Luke began, 'but in medieval times when they started to build a house it was the custom to bury in the foundations the corpse of an animal, a cat often or even a hare or a rat, the superstition being that this would bring luck to the future dwelling and its occupants. The story goes – and it is well-authenticated – that when this house was begun it was a cat that they buried in the wall, a dead cat no doubt, but one that when alive had been the familiar of a local witch known as Green Margery.'

'She wasn't really a witch, was she?' said Spinny.

'The people here believed she was. They believed in her when, having discovered that the builders had taken her cat and killed it and buried it in the wall, she put a curse on this house. She predicted that the cat would haunt the house for as long as it stood or until its skeleton was unearthed – wherever it might be.'

I asked him what became of her, more to amuse Spinny than out of real interest.

'Matthew Hopkins, he they called the Witchfinder General, came here from Essex and hunted her out and they had a trial and Green Margery was hanged. I know no more than that, not even the precise dates nor where Green Margery lived, nor,' and here Luke smiled at Spinny, 'what kind of a cat it was.'

'It's a black cat,' said Spinny.

Was Luke deceiving me? Oh, I do not mean over this matter of witches and cats. Did he ever lie to me as to where he was in the evenings? I think not. Only if to tell half the truth and leave out the rest is to lie. The doors to his mind he must have closed against me and I did not know the magic word that would cause them to swing open, did not at that time even know they were closed and imagined that the thoughts I read, Greek pentameters, theological speculation, were all the thoughts he had. When I was aware of the doors closing I imagined in my innocence that the room inside them was the place where he worried about *me*, that he was preoccupied with a particular concern about, say, my health. Of the occupancy of someone else in that hidden chamber I had not the faintest suspicion.

The guests to the dinner party we were to give, Luke invited himself. That should have made me wary but it did not. I supposed he thought me too young at sixteen to issue invitations, or rather that our guests would think me too young. He told me whom he intended to ask. We were sitting in the study on opposite sides of the desk, about to begin our *Antigone* reading, I only too willing to abandon Edgar Allen Poe when Luke called me to something far more intellectually demanding.

He opened the book. 'Before I forget,' he said, 'I must let you know whom I've asked to dinner. Dr and Mrs Cyprian, as a matter of course, and Dr Trewynne, and two of our faculty members you don't know, Dr Bulmer and Dr Leonard.'

I remember thinking that half the company might have worn scarlet if it chose – such a plethora of PhDs! Then (in my innocence) I thought that the men might outnumber the women. But I hardly cared. I was anxious to start our reading. It was ironic the line with which I began, Antigone's response to Creon;

'There is death in that remark: the sound of death.'

Sheila came to cook for the dinner party but she had very little to do, for Luke bought stuff like smoked salmon and strawberries that simply had to be put on plates. I do not remember what our main course was. Food bores me. So do clothes, as I have already said, but one must wear them and when Spinny said she wanted us to be dressed alike, of course I acquiesced. Identical white dresses we already possessed, made for our confirmations, hers a month before, mine three years past. It still fitted, was even rather loose on me, though the hem which had reached to mid-calf was now on my knees. We wore blue sashes, made from a skirt belonging to our mother that we tore into strips and turned the frayed edges to the inside. I cannot sew. Spinny has grown a lot in the past year and her head is up past my shoulder. Her brown curls hang to the middle of her back and that evening my long fair hair, newly washed and brushed, covered me like a golden cape.

Rosemary was there to answer the door. It spoils things a little, I believe, if one has to go to the door oneself. I asked her to wear a white apron but she unaccountably refused.

'You may be living in the eighteen hundreds,' she said very rudely, 'but the rest of us aren't. The days of slavery are past.'

It was a beautiful evening and the french windows were open on to our walled garden. Luke's narcissi came from our garden and in April there are scyllas there too and tiny species of tulips, but in summer no flowers grow there but roses. Mermaid and Golden Showers and Albertine cover the walls while in the beds grow the loveliest of hybrid teas, such floribundas as Allotria and Europeana, William Lobb the moss rose and Agnes the rugosa hybrid. The sky was not cloudless but flecked all over as if with tiny rose feathers and beyond the flower-hung walls could be seen the west front of our cathedral, its towers taller than those of Wells and therefore giving an impression of greater symmetry and balance, its niches supporting no less than four hundred and twenty-two figures of angels and archangels and apostles and saints, bathed in declining but still radiant sunlight.

We stood waiting for our guests, the three of us. My mind went to Victorian problem pictures once more, fancying that we again resembled such a one, 'The Widower and his Daughters' perhaps, for I thought I detected something careworn and anxious in Luke's face as he stood between us, Spinny and me in our white dresses, each with a gold cross on a thin chain around our necks. Later I understood that it was a look of fear and that it was of me he was afraid.

Dr and Mrs Cyprian were the first to arrive. He is a minor canon who attempts a youthful contemporary look by sporting sidewhiskers and wearing his hair long, but succeeds only in looking like a character out of Trollope. She is one of those women who bedizen themselves. Every inch of her is decorated, from her highlighted hair and painted eyes to her white lace stockings and narrow strap sandals, so high that she must perforce rock and prance in them like a mettlesome mare. We all permitted ourselves to be kissed in that passive way one must and fortunately my flinching passed unnoticed, for at that moment Rosemary announced Dr Trewynno. He is our GP, a bachelor of medicine, not a true doctor at all, and he fixed me at once with his censorious leech's eye.

'If you go on like this, Elvira,' he said, 'we shall have you fading away. Let me recommend a glass of this excellent Oloroso.'

Smilingly I declined. He crammed a fistful of tiger nuts into his mouth.

'Seriously, my dear, it wouldn't be a bad idea for you to come and see my at the surgery one of these fine evenings. Ring up for an appointment and I'll fit you in after my other patients. What do you say?'

'That it might not be a bad idea but nor would it be a good one. I think we could call it a *specious* idea.' I was rather pleased with that.

'Sometimes I think you're growing even more pedantic and precious than your old dad,' he said – rudely, I think, since he was drinking Luke's sherry.

The doorbell rang and I remember recalling that of course we had two more guests to come, those faculty members, Dr Bulmer and Dr Leonard. Rosemary showed them in without announcing them. She did not know their names as she did Dr Trewynne's and presumably would have considered it a slave's part to enquire. Luke, who had been talking to Mrs Cyprian on the terrace, positively ran back into the room, ran with unseemly haste. The man, Dr Bulmer – Alan is his christian name – made no impression on me whatsoever. He is a cipher, pale, small, myopic, shy. The woman – for the other guest, the last of our guests, was a woman – what can I say of her? Volumes or nothing. At present nothing, only that she was young, no more than nine or ten years older than I, and that from the first moment I saw her I knew who and what she was and why she was here.

I knew it from Luke's embarrassment and care and fear. Involuntarily, I believe, for he had lost control, he allowed the doors of his mind to burst open and me to read what lay within. It was so clear that I wonder all those present did not read it, the passions and unwise desires blazoned in fiery letters, but they could not, they did not. Their faces remained as they had been, polite, enquiring, mildly interested, Spinny's so sweetly inno-cent and unsuspecting that I felt in the midst of my pain a hot lava-like eruption of love for her.

Yes, it was pain. I will describe what it was like. It was as if my soul had become one of those limestone figures on the west front of our cathedral and some restorer, incompetent at his craft, was chipping away at it with a

27

sharp tool, flaying its surface and splintering off those soft perceptive parts so that at last only a plain featureless nothing would remain. I could feel flakes of my soul falling about me, each shard shed with agony and myself, the core of me, growing refined and tenuous, becoming a mere shadow. I was afraid I would faint.

I held out a cold hand to her. I heard Luke speak her name.

'This is Mary Leonard.'

What is there in him that draws him to these little women with little names? Anne first, now Mary.

'I hear you are a great classical scholar,' were the first words she spoke to me.

I smiled. That is, I drew my lips apart and stretched them to each side, exposing my teeth.

'And versatile too if you are cooking dinner for all of us.'

'A woman comes to do that,' I said through my wide smile and my bared teeth.

I have very little recollection of the conversation, still less of what we ate. I spoke not a word to my neighbours, Dr Trewynne and Alan Bulmer. Subjects under discussion droned about me, swooped and twittered like birds of passage and birds of prey: our ghosts, the restoration of the cathedral's west front, Mrs Cyprian's new car, some promising undergraduate who was a favourite of both Luke and Bulmer. *She*, I remember, spoke flatteringly, unctuously, about the food, the room, the house. Under my breath I repeated over and over, though Dr Trewynne's eyes were fixed curiously on me:

'There is death in that remark, the sound of death.'

Two weeks later to the day, when the roses were past

their best and Agnes was over for another summer, Luke told us he was going to marry Mary Leonard. He called us both into the study and said he had something to tell us. Spinny had somehow got it into her head we were going to move house, a change she would have welcomed because of the ghosts. I knew better. I had known from the moment she set foot in our drawing room and he smiled in a special way and held her hand a great deal longer than he had held Mrs Cyprian's.

He began by asking us if we liked her. I decided not to lie. Is it not odd that there is no prohibition on lying in the Ten Commandments? Perhaps this is because it is hard to say why lying is wrong, though easy enough to know how often it can be degrading. Deciding not to lie, I said nothing. Spinny said she liked her. She liked her eyes, if you please! For my part I had noticed nothing about her eyes except that they were small and had lids to them and rather short lashes.

'She's an intellectual,' he said. 'She was just twenty-five when she was awarded her doctorate. The subject of her thesis was building and masonry techniques in the thirteenth century. She is already a distinguished medievalist.'

It was for her mind then that he loved her. It must have been, for what else had she? But it pierced me to the soul that he loved her for her mind. I would have fallen on my knees and begged him not to do it but my dignity, my idea of myself, held me back.

'I have asked her to marry me and she has said yes.'

As if any woman born would have said no to him!

Spinny looked delighted, as if she had been promised an outing or a present. She went to him and put her arms round his neck. He knew me better than to expect a similar demonstration. Her favours were cheap, were nothing, and though he let her cling to him it was at me that he looked, sweat on his lip, his eyes pleading, the way I hated to see him. Before I spoke to him an earthquake or curious revolution took place in my mind and was succeeded by a great calm. She would never come to this house as his wife, she would never be married to him, she or anyone else, ever. How absurd I had been to see a threat where no threat existed, where no threat could be!

Of course I did not kiss him or touch him. I said, and it was with all my heart, my voice rich with love: 'I give you my very best wishes for your future happiness, Luke.'

I meant that and seeing I meant it, he smiled with joyful relief. So I went Grimya away and we began to read the Fifth Episode.

'How it goes against the grain
To smother all one's heart's desire!
I cannot fight with destiny.'

At last I closed the book and said good-night to him. He put out his hand to me and I think he wanted me to kiss him but smiling, I shook my head ever so slightly. Outside the closed door I stood waiting for a moment, listening. I heard him lift the phone and dial and presently say in a way that was gentle yet breathless: 'Darling...?'

Half-way down the long passage which runs through our house on the second floor I made out a dark shape, crouched, sphynx-like. It rose up on the tips of its paws, arched its back and darted away as I approached. All our windows were open, for it was a hot night, and the Cyprians' cat could have got in when it pleased, but I had not realised its coat was such a dark colour. As it disappeared round the turn that leads to the back stairs a wailing cry came from Spinny's room.

I ran in. She was sitting up in bed with her arms out.

'I heard the voice,' she cried. 'I heard the whispering voice. It said, Despina, Despina, Despina....'

It was the day after Luke told us he was going to re-marry and Spinny heard the whispering voice that I began writing all these things down. Before that I had only written stories, Gothic tales really, in the manner of Clara Reeve and Ann Radclyffe, but I exhausted all my ideas and it was partly for lack of subject matter that I turned my attention to real life, our lives. I wrote and wrote until I was weary and then I laid aside my pen and read, steeping myself for escape in the works of Edgar Allan Poe whom I had not long discovered. I wonder if Poe has affected my style?

It cannot matter anyway, for Poe is a great writer and famous. I love his long sentences and polysyllabic words, his glooms and his glories. But if I read at this rate I shall have finished the *Tales of Mystery and Imagination* in a day or two, and shall have nothing for consolation and escape unless I go back to the beginning of the collection. Postponing for a while the pleasure Poe brings me, I shall return to my account of us, of Luke and me and Spinny and Mary Leonard.

Especially Mary Leonard. It is time I described her. She is small with silky brown hair and skin excessively freckled. My grandmother once had a Dalmatian that was said not to be a good specimen because its spots were all run together instead of being distinct and separate. Mary Leonard's freckles are like that Dalmatian's spots, all run together. Apart from that, she is rather pretty and she is thin, not one of those women who show the shape of their breasts through their clothes. But she has holes in her ear lobes and stubble on her legs. Her legs are like a cornfield that has just been cut and before they burn it off. I look at Mary Leonard's legs and imagine setting fire to the stubble with a match.

'I wonder why he wants to marry,' I said to Spinny. 'He cannot be lonely. He has me.'

'He has *us*,' said Spinny.

She makes me impatient sometimes. 'He has us, then. So it isn't loneliness. Nor can it be a housekeeper he wants, for Rosemary and Sheila do all that and besides Mary Leonard told me she cannot so much as boil an egg.'

'He wants to have sexual intercourse with her,' said Spinny.

I shrank into myself at that. I shuddered. Of course I do not *believe* her, for it is my father we were talking of, who is surely a sexless being as angels are said to be, but that she should harbour such thoughts, that such an answer should present itself to her as obvious, as taken for granted! I treasure my virginity and always shall. *Her* mind, that I have never claimed to read, must be a place where slimy things swim and jostle, pale-eyed, as in some subterranean sink. And she seemed, smiling, to relish the thought of Luke and Mary Leonard together. It is true that she likes this woman, responding to her overtures with a show of affection. Poor fool, she still misses our mother and thinks it possible to replace her. And her nights, then, were still bad. She still saw the cat and heard the voice whispering her name. At last I went to see Dr Trewynne, making an appointment for a consultation after his regular patients had gone, as he has asked me to do on the night we first met Mary Leonard.

'So you've finally honoured me with a visit, Elvira,' he said in that facetious tone people of his age often use when they speak to me. 'And none too soon, I should say. How much do you weigh? Do you know?'

I dismissed this with a wave of my hand and said that I had come about Spinny. She could not sleep and I wanted to give her something to make her sleep. The ghosts I naturally did not mention. Could he supply her with a soporific?

'Now wait a minute, young lady. Hold your horses.'

He went on like this for a while. I sat there wondering if I could steal one of the leaves off his prescription pad, if I could get him out of the room for an instant to do this, for by then I had decided I must regard the means as justified by the end. However, he showed no signs of even getting to his feet and eventually he said he would come and see Spinny and if he felt it was justified, prescribe for her a mild sedative.

At home I found Mary Leonard, ostensibly helping Spinny with her history essay. She was going through the two or three pages covered in Spinny's immature rounded hand (large and sprawling to use up the maximum amount of paper), sometimes putting her head on one side, raising her eyebrows and looking quizzically at poor little Spinny before asking her some question more suitable for a postgraduate. When she wants to call Spinny or summon her – sometimes when she simply wants to address her across the room – Mary Leonard sings her name in the way, she says, certain characters in *Cosi Fan Tutte* sing it during a sextet.

'O Despina! Olà, Despina!'

She knows the operas of Mozart at least as well as our mother did. Spinny smiles uneasily when sung at like this and Mary Leonard tells her she should respond with: 'Le padrone!'

Which means, of course, 'the mistresses'. These mistresses, no doubt, are Mary Leonard and myself, for it is my response and my affection she would have. Spinny is too easily won, too willing a captive. And anyway she never responds, she cannot sing, like me she is tone deaf. That evening, when I had been to the doctor and walked home through the soft summer dusk, when I found my wistful sister looking for love to that woman she thought would be her stepmother and that woman singing her name and lecturing her on the Peasants' Revolt, Mary Leonard also sang to me.

'Elvira, idol' mio,' she sang with many a fancy trill.

Not even once did I let this pass.

'Oblige me by never in any circumstances doing that again.'

She turned pale and the freckles stood out in dark blotches. Oh, she is no beauty and Spinny must be, must be wrong! Mary Leonard attempted a laugh.

'I mean it,' I said

'You're being absurd, Elvira.'

'I don't care to be mocked in my own house,' I said. 'You'll find that teasing in any form is not welcome here.'

34

She only smiled and looked to catch Luke's eye, but Luke had quietly left the room before our exchange began. However, she sang no more to me and began instead to flatter and cajole me, suggesting, if you please, that I should be her bridesmaid, a grotesque notion which Luke has put a stop to. But why me when this was a role which would have brought such happiness to Spinny? My little sister's lip trembled and her eyes filled with tears and later Mary Leonard did say: 'You too, of course, Despina.'

But by then it was too late, the whole plan having come under the inexorable edict of Luke's veto.

They are to be married in September in the cathedral and the Dean will perform the ceremony. Or so they believe. They are undeterred by the knowledge that from 1st September the whole west front of the cathedral will be covered in scaffolding for the restoration work which is due to begin a week later. Nor do they suspect other hindrances. I know it will never take place and am seeking about for means to prevent it.

Poison I should like. Those Renaissance notions of poisoning appeal to me, poisoning with a ring, a glove, a fan, though I know that such recourse will be impossible to me, whereas drugs, dull latter-day substitutes, may not be. Dr Trewynne has been to see Spinny, examined her and talked to her and left a prescription for some kind of tranquilliser. I am giving a lot of thought to how I can persuade him to produce something stronger.... Poe might help me, I thought, and I have read *Ligeia* and *Berenice* and *Morella*, though not to much avail. I have talked to Spinny about it, unwilling to do anything she might not share in, wanting to make it a concerted effort.

The Greeks said that Hera had ox eyes and they meant it as a compliment. Today we should hardly think it flattering. Spinny has those bovine eyes, large, dark brown, glowing, docile. They were fixed upon my face and her lips were a little parted, drops of sweat on her low broad forehead like dew. She leaned forward and she was trembling as I spoke of capsules opened and the powder they contained dropped in drinks, of a fall from one of our high windows, of a wasp sting in the mouth...

She covered her ears with her hands.

'I don't want to hear! I don't want to hear!'

And then I was presented with a gift. She came to stay with us. Mary Leonard moved into our house. The practical facts of people's lives mean so little to me – where they live and how they live and what money they have – that I had taken no note of her provenance. She had a room or flat, I believe, some kind of dwelling somewhere in the city. I have overheard her telling Spinny about it, Spinny who sat wide-eyed, greedy (for some unaccountable reason) for those details of domestic husbandry she had never before heard at home. Later on my sister tried to regale me with anecdotes of meter readings, telephone accounts, landladies and removal costs.

In a parody of her own behaviour, I put my hands over my ears.

'I don't want to hear,' I said.

'She has to leave her flat. She's going to come here until they're married.'

'They will never be married,' I said.

Luke had said nothing to me but had himself instructed Rosemary to get one of our spare rooms ready.

He has grown remote from me, withdrawn himself and closed the shutters on his thoughts, but once she is dead I know he will come back. His love for me, his *oneness* with me, will even be strengthened. And he will see his desire to marry this woman as a frightful aberration, a kind of midsummer madness, from which her timely death has saved him. The scales will fall from his eyes. I see Luke's eyes as covered with a cataract-like layer of silver scales resembling the glittering thick armour of a fish, and this carapace will fall or melt away at the touch of my fingers to disclose the clear-sighted brilliant blue orbs beneath. But now he wears the scales like a mask that has changed him from my beloved father into an ordinary misguided besotted man.

Yesterday she came. It is already August and I have no clear plan or strategy yet but I will have, I will.

It has happened and I was the perpetrator, I must have been. If only I could remember more clearly. I am setting these things down to help me remember. My mind has become like a carpet woven in many colours and an intricate pattern but the loom on which it is stretched has been broken, the warp and the weft torn down, and the thousand threads inextricably intermingled. How shall I begin to disentangle them?

I would rather return to Poe and forget but I must not. I must try to go back to that day when she came, or the day after, or the night I first watched her through the floor, early in August, the beginning of the second week of that hot dry month.

Rosemary had given her the room directly below mine. There was a hole in its ceiling through which an electric lead passed, for being so old, our house is full of cracks and holes of this kind. I examined it before Mary Leonard moved in and in the floor above the hole, in my own room, I raised the carpet and lifted up a board so that I could see quite clearly anything that might take place below. I would be able to look down on Mary Leonard asleep in bed.

I told Spinny, for I had no secrets from her.

'You are like Catherine de Medici,' she said.

It surprised me Spinny had ever heard of her but then I remembered historical romances are her favourite reading matter. 'Why so?' I said smiling at her.

'She used to look through a crack in the floorboards at Henri Deux making love with Diane de Poitiers. Henri,' she said, 'was Catherine's husband.'

'I know that, thank you,' I said, my voice shaking with disgust.

Spinny is of the earth earthy, not to say of the flesh fleshy. She said:

'He won't go in there anyway. He's saving that till after they're married.'

'Do you imagine I suspect him of *that*? Do you think that is why I want to see in there?'

Apparently she did, strange little creature. Mary Leonard had told her she meant to bring with her her record player (she called it a 'music centre' as if it were some kind of shop) and play on it long-playing records of the operas of Mozart.

'Even Mother wasn't allowed to do that,' said Spinny.

This strengthened my resolution to do away with her. I have wondered since if it could have been the power of my thoughts and my determination alone which frayed, dislodged, upset a certain balance.... Or was it more? I do not know, yet I must come to know. Not on the first but on the second night she slept in our house I looked down through the floor into her bedroom. She slept with the windows wide open and Mrs Cyprian's cat had come in and was lying asleep on the petit point cover of a long stool. There was a wasps' nest under the eaves just above me and I thought it unwise to leave the windows like that. The man would be coming in a day or two to kill the wasps with cyanide in a long spoon. Moonlight streamed in and fell in a cold silvery bar across her face. She slept on her back with her mouth open. Of course she was quite young and pretty enough and her teeth were good, so this was not as offensive as it might have been in an older person. There was a cup on the table beside her which had contained some bedtime drink.

The next night I watched her again and the next and the next. I could not see how it might be managed, the mechanics of it, though the plan was clear enough in my mind. Once, in the following week, I watched all night, lying on the bedroom floor, my head pressed down into the area between the joists and the ceiling below, my eye to the hole. For hours I lay like that, staring down. She stirred and moved, she turned over, she was not at all a sound sleeper. The moon was waning and its light less bright than the last time I had watched, so I could not see so clearly. It would soon be September, yet the dawn still came early and it was light at five. The buzzing of a wasp awakened her. She got up, caught the wasp in her cup, put it outside and closed the window.

Was it because I had lain awake watching her all night that I fainted the next morning? It could not have been lack of food as I had been eating something almost every day. Certainly that marked the beginning of my feelings of weakness and enfeeblement, as if I were somehow departing from my physical self. I was arranging flowers in a vase on Luke's desk, a task I still meticulously performed for him, though he never thanked me, still less removed a blossom from the arrangement to lay by his left hand. They were white asters, I remember, and a succulent with coppery red leaves and flat bracts of pink flowers. As I took the last aster in my hand and stood looking at my handiwork, in doubt exactly where the flower should be placed, a dizziness overcame me, the light and colours darkened and turned black and I fell to the floor.

Spinny came running in.

'What's the matter with you? What's happened?'

I had been unconscious for only a few seconds. Spinny bent over me with staring eyes and her mouth half-open. I asked her to bring me a glass of water. Almost immediately after this the wasp man arrived. He is from a village a few miles outside the city and every summer he comes to us to kill our wasps. Why Luke never called in the local authority I cannot say. We always use the wasp man. Each time he comes he cautions us about the chemicals he uses, prussic acid, potassium cyanide, telling us as if we are half-witted children not to approach within a yard of it. Where he gets it and how he is allowed to possess it I have never known, and very likely he is not allowed but has illegal access to its source.

The implement he uses is a long metal rod with a metal bowl on the end of it, rather bigger than a thimble. This he fills with cyanide and, placing his ladder against the house, climbs up and tips the contents of the 'spoon' into the guttering under the eaves or into the wasps' nest itself and the approaches to it if he can reach them. Still feeling weak, my head swimming, I watched his preparation, something I have never done before.

He keeps the cyanide in an old rusty tin. He took out the requisite amount, replaced the lid on the tin and put it back in the canvas bag which he carried with him. This he left on the floor in the back of his van. As soon as he was out of sight I put on a pair of Rosemary's household gloves and tied a handkerchief round my face. Helping myself to a spoonful out of the tin, I put it into a cup and thence into a small jar I found in one of the kitchen cupboards. Half-way through this stealthy procedure and the transfer of the chemical which took place in my room, I became aware that Spinny was watching me. She had followed me upstairs and stood in the doorway, staring with what may have been distress but was probably only wonder. She said nothing and I offered no explanation. She even saw where I hid the cyanide, behind the classical dictionaries on the bookshelf in my bedroom.

It was about a week after this that Mary Leonard died.

The scaffolding went up on the west front of the cathedral and very disfiguring it is. Until this happened I had not realised how much this beautiful sight, so close to our windows, has meant in my life; the serenity and majesty of it, its glory at sunset, its unearthly loveliness when the moon shines, the curious effect snow has, fitting little white caps on to the figures and frosting their wings. Our west front has been called a gigantic open-air

41

reredos and only purists have found it inferior to Reims or Chartres.

I had not understood how totally the scaffolding would obscure it and I watched with despondency the metal poles and planking and rope handrails going up. The figures are all to be cleaned, all those in need of it restored and the crumbling carvings of the Apostles Peter and Paul who stand in the gabled niche above the great west door replaced by modern sculpture.

The overall effect from a distance was what I had always enjoyed seeing. But as soon as she understood that the scaffolding would make certain of the carved figures accessible, Mary Leonard was wild to go up there and look more closely. This was natural, for the rich surface display had all been placed there during her particular period, that is between 1210 and 1240. Luke would not have dreamed of scaling the west front without permission but this the Dean quite willingly gave and it was decided that we should all go up on the Saturday afternoon which would be the first Saturday in September and exactly two weeks before the date set for Luke and Mary Leonard's wedding.

She had a red dress on. Luke and she held hands but he dropped hers when the Dean and Dr Cyprian came up to us – out of decorousness, I suppose. It was misguided of her, but Spinny who is quite big and plump now, had put on a white broderie anglaise blouse with her jeans and sandals and Mary Leonard called her 'la belle Despinetta'. She was a woman given to teasing and mockery and undeterred by the failure of this particular quip, she told Dr Cyprian that he looked just like the Archangel Michael up there, for their hair was the same length and equally sparse. Only Luke smiled, shaking an admonitory finger at her.

We climbed up, making our way along the lowest catwalk to look at the original Apostles who were still there at that time. Then we climbed to the next level which passes across the centre of the 'open-air reredos' so that we might examine the windows, just one of which contains stained glass pre-dating Cromwell. On the third level are eight gabled niches, four containing figures of the four archangels, four displaying, as if flying from the gates of heaven, six-winged seraphim. These, all for some reason in a good state of preservation, were of great interest to Mary Leonard, in particular Michael whom, after making some learned and to the rest of us incomprehensible remarks about him, she once more compared to Dr Cyprian. But what she most wanted to see at close quarters were the Twelve Disciples who, with Christ in the midst of them, sit at supper in a long stone bay between the two vast flanking towers. The fourth and topmost catwalk runs at a level with their feet and at a height of some hundred and twenty feet from the ground.

Up we went. I began to feel a little dizzy, from all that climbing perhaps, but I said nothing. Mary Leonard ran along ahead of me in her haste to see the statuary and the Dean called out to us to be careful, to keep our wits about us, for although there were wooden uprights attached to the planking, the handrail was merely a length of stout rope.

Since then greater precautions have been taken to ensure the safety of these catwalks. The coroner at the inquest on Mary Leonard censured the Dean for taking us up there at all. The frayed rope was not much commented on. It was assumed that an inferior length of rope had been used at this particular point, something, it was suggested, which would have been of no account if only experienced workmen had used the catwalk. What had possessed the Dean to take his friends, including women and children, up there?

The Dean was not even looking when it happened. Exactly where Luke and Dr Cyprian were I do not know. I hardly know where I was or Spinny, but I do remember seeing Mary Leonard stop in front of the figures and step back and look up, stare up with her head raised heavenwards. Did I touch her, push her, or was it the frayed rope alone that led to her death? I cannot tell, my mind has emptied itself of remembered actions and when I look back over these few weeks I see only the intensely blue sky with the tower soaring into the shimmer of it, a flock of white birds flying at dazzling height, the seated figures with their faces all rubbed away by weather and by time. And I see Mary Leonard in her red dress standing tiptoe . . . .

When she fell I was not looking. She screamed in the air. Luke cried out and ran and for a moment flattened himself against the Disciples' feet, his mouth a great O of agony. That I remember and the sound her body made when it struck the ground, a crash that was both hard and soft at the same time. She lay down there on the stones we call hearts and whether there was blood or not I cannot say, for her dress was too red to show it.

A frightful tragedy, everyone said, a brilliant mind, a young life, such promise, everything before her! Mrs

Cyprian has called and said how she feels for us in our loss, she can think of nothing else. She actually cried as she spoke and the blue stuff ran off her eyelids down her face, and her earrings which were tiny yellow birds in gilded cages shook about, jingling.

Her cat has been in Spinny's room again.

'Would you please stop that animal of yours coming into our house?' I said to her as politely as I could.

She took immediate umbrage and defended herself with a lie. The cat had been shut up in their kitchen for eight hours.

'On the contrary,' I said, 'it was in my sister's room all night.'

There was no answer she could make to that, so she took refuge in insult.

'Your poor father. I pity *him*.'

So do I, though for a different reason. Infatuated with Mary Leonard as he had been, he took her loss with great suffering. Evening after evening we sat in silence together in his study, a silence he broke only to tell me of some aspect of Mary Leonard's character which had especially entranced him, even some aspect of her looks. But it was her mind he dwelt on most persistently, a mind he said that had been nearly equal to his own. Where could he find such another woman? It was impossible. Except in me, he said, except in his elder daughter, and on me he fixed his eyes with an expression of yearning piteous tenderness.

Alone again after these painful confrontations, I have asked myself over and over if it is I who have been responsible for causing him this pain and this loss. But when I make this enquiry my mind seems to close up and instead of memory I am presented with a picture, a kind of collage composed of many and varied pieces, the refulgent blue sky, the grey-gold stone, Mary Leonard's blood-red dress and the brown cobbles that are the size and shape of human hearts.

But if I cannot remember that afternoon I can recall all too well my intention to kill her. The cyanide in its little jar is still to be found behind the classical dictionaries in my bedroom, bearing witness to my intention. For weeks the carpet on my bedroom floor remained folded back, the floorboard beneath it removed. In my bedroom too, still there, are a cup and a spoon for catching a wasp and a piece of gauze to cover the cup and let the wasp breathe. Which particular method of disposing of Mary Leonard I should choose I had not decided on. Did I ever decide? Or did I reject these others in favour of a plan which Mary Leonard's own wishes in the matter of climbing the west front of the cathedral suggested to me? How dizzy I had felt up there, how vague and vulnerable, seized by a half-real, half-imagined vertigo. Yet I had wanted her dead and, standing there on the catwalk, she had surely put her life into my hands. There is something else as well. When it was all over and her body was taken away and the people had gone and Luke been given things to make him sleep, I went to my room and found in the pocket of my dress a penknife. I unfolded it and saw on one of the blades fibres that might have come from rope.

I want to be old but I do not want to be a woman, I want to be a scholar but not a student, I want to be an intellectual, an author, a success, an authority, but I do not want the labour that must precede all this. There is no one to whom I can tell these things but I can write them down. This winter, this spring, I have hardly been to school. Spinny told me I was breaking the law but I answered her that school is not obligatory when one is over sixteen and she said no more.

Luke, I think, has not noticed. He is too unhappy. For a long time he scarcely spoke to us and seemed to look through us as if we were transparent. No more work has been done on 'Noogenesis' and even Newman cannot comfort him. Nights are the best time for him, for he has his barbiturates to make him sleep. Dr Trewynne hardly hesitated before prescribing him the powerful sedative I had once requested for Spinny. Then, a little over a month ago he emerged from his lethargy to suggest that he and I read *The Medea* together, a work that up till then we had for some reason neglected. I had just read that passage that mocks the consolations of literature:

'None of those poets has discovered
How to put an end with their singing
To grief, bitter grief . . .'

I had just read it when he interrupted me and saying he had a letter he wanted me to see, took a sheet of paper from one of the drawers of his desk. It was in Luke's own handwriting, that exemplary calligraphy which is as beautiful to look at as it is easy to read, and it was addressed to me. He called me his 'dearest daughter Elvira' and bade me take care of my younger sister, intellectually my inferior and young for her years. Our mother was not mentioned. His own mother he referred to only in expressing his understanding of what sorrow it must be to lose a child....

47

At this point I understood the purpose of the letter and gave a cry of protest.

'Read it all,' said Luke, 'before you say anything.'

I was cold and my hands were shaking but I read on. His daughters would leave him, he had written, and their departure not be long deferred. On Mary Leonard he had built all his hopes of happiness and now Mary Leonard was dead, life had lost all its meaning and he saw no reason to continue it. He intended to die quietly and in the least alarming way possible, causing the least inconvenience to anyone. Everything he possessed he had left to his daughters, in trust until each had reached the age of eighteen.

'You won't do this, will you?' I said. 'You would not have shown it to me if you had meant to do it.'

He smiled sadly at me and shook his head. No, he would not do it, not now. He was a clergyman, he was a father, he had certain responsibilities.

'I fancy loving parents often write such letters at times of depression or fear,' he said. 'I know my own mother wrote such a letter to me when she was expecting my brother and feared she might die in childbirth.' He took the letter from me and replaced it in the drawer. 'Come, let us return to *The Medea*. Poetry may be a solace in this life when nothing else can be, whatever Euripides may say to the contrary.'

That night I hardly slept. Life without Luke is unimaginable. Unless – unless he and I might die together. Has there ever in the whole of history been a suicide pact between a father and a daughter? It is the kind of thing Poe might have written of but I do not think he did. How strange that though I read his stories so recently I have almost forgotten them, along with so much else I have learned, though I have a confused memory, like a protracted complex dream, of those tales of his in which emaciated dying black-haired mysterious women are inextricably mingled with demons, eccentrics, phantasms, grotesques and mad doctors in rooms designed as torture chambers.

Some few days – or weeks perhaps – after this I told Spinny everything. It was somewhat against my inclinations to tell her, but I need her help in keeping a constant watch on Luke at least until this current depression of his has passed. I am taking my A levels and have to be away from the house on examination days.

'I wish I could live in an ordinary family!' Spinny burst out.

'What on earth do you mean?' I said.

'I wish mother hadn't died. Why did she have to die? Why do we have to call our father by his christian name and have Greek and Latin lessons with him? I hate it, I hate this house, it's full of ghosts and I'm afraid of ghosts. I'm afraid of the cat and the lady's footsteps and the voice that calls my name. Why do we have to live here? Do you know what I should like? I don't suppose you care but I'm going to tell you just the same. I should like to live with Granny in her house and have my friends to stay and play records and be *ordinary*.'

She is such a child. Of course it hardly matters if she takes time off school to watch Luke, for she is doing very badly there. Her work has fallen off dreadfully this past year. I am fortunate that anxiety and stress seem to have a very different effect on me and although I am not well, although I am very weak and prone to attacks of giddiness, I am finding these examinations child's play. This morning a letter came offering me a place at St

Leofric's Hall, consequent of course upon my examination results, but as Luke says, that is a mere formality in my case.

I am lying in the garden in a long chair. I have been here for most of the day. It has been the first beautiful day of summer, the sky cloudless and the sun very warm and bright. The buds on Allotria and Europeana and Albertine, the climbing rose, which were still closed this morning, have been coaxed open by the sunshine during the course of the day. Rosemary, who has just come out here to bring me a cup of coffee and a shortbread biscuit (which I cannot imagine eating) says it is the beginning of a heatwave. I have moved my chair back into the shade, though any effort of this sort makes me breathless. Climbing stairs is the worst thing and it is easiest for me to go up them on all-fours. One night last week Spinny came out of her bedroom and stood there looking at me.

'I thought I heard the lady,' she said. 'I thought I heard the swish of her skirts but it was you. It was your legs rubbing against the carpet. I think you're mad.'

'Do you indeed?' I said.

'If Mother had lived she would have made you eat. I'm going to tell Gran about you and how you don't eat anything. And I'm going to ask Luke to send me to boarding school.'

Whether she had made the latter appeal I don't know. Luke and I are estranged, for one evening a few days after this I offended him deeply. Tired and worn, I laid my head against the back of the settee where we were sitting and trying desperately to appreciate to the uttermost his thundering out of some great speech Euripides had given to Menelaus, I fell into an apathetic doze.

Luke's voice, crisp and peevish, awoke me.

'Come now Elvira, I think I have better things to do with my time than waste it on a young woman who frivols away the day so that she is too exhausted for work in the evening.'

I apologised to him, seeing the justice of what he said, though I had spent the day lying in this chair here in the garden.

But nothing upsets him so much as apparent indifference. Nothing is so displeasing to him as being ignored.

'Perhaps we had better have no more readings until you have decided which takes precedence, adolescent pastimes or Euripides.'

Why does this distress me so little? Very little seems to interest or concern me, and though I am writing again I hardly know what I am writing. When I read I fall asleep over the book.

Yesterday Grandmother came. The weather was cooler than today and we were indoors, Spinny and I, she sullen and cross, for Luke has told her she will not be allowed to go out alone with Tom, her new boyfriend, but that they must, if they please, take me along. I do not quite see myself in the role of watchful chaperone, even supposing I were strong enough....

'Let me take you to Dr Trewynne,' Grandmother said. 'I think you should be in hospital.'

'Oh, no,' I said, smiling a little, smiling the way I once smiled at Mary Leonard. 'Oh, no,' and I raised one arm to wave her away.

I realised she and Spinny were looking at the skin of

my upper arm, once white and smooth. It has been puzzling me too, the fine golden down that has grown all over me, the lanugo that covers every inch of my body except the palms of my hands and the soles of my feet. I am furred like a lean cat.

'She's dying of starvation!' Spinny cried and she threw herself on me, clutching me in her arms.

I tried to hold her off. The Chinese complain about the smell of those who eat butter and cream and cheese and I know what they mean. Poor Spinny cried and her face got red and swollen and Grandmother said she would have a consultation with Luke to see what should be done about me.

It is true that I am dying. Indifference tells me so. I care for no one any more, not even for Luke – much. I take no interest in the future, for I cannot see beyond this day, this night. Here is a paradox. I set out to ignore the body and mortify it so that I might be all spirit, and I have done so, I have wasted the flesh and thinned the blood so that when I hold up my hand to the setting sun I see the light penetrate skin and bone, tendons and veins, with a glow that is the creamy-pink of an Albertine rose. But in doing so I have thinned and drained the spirit too, for it would seem that the soul depends on the body for its existence. Mine, at any rate, has lost its vigour along with the body's vigour, its ability to leap and tower and transcend. There is nothing much left but weariness and a longing for rest.

The light is fast going and as it dies the perfume of the air increases, the scent of roses and honeysuckle and white philadelphus. Bees move sluggishly towards their hives and dusky moths come out to seek the light. They flutter towards Luke's window, a square of orange on the dark house wall. I lie here, looking up at that bright square, wondering why Luke, who always opens his window on fine nights before he sleeps, should tonight have left it closed.

Why should I not sleep out here all night? Who will know or care? Luke went off to bed soon after Spinny brought him his evening drink. She brought one to me too and I can see the milky puddle, fast soaking away into the dry earth, that it made when I poured it away.

It is too dark to read now and Poe has fallen on the grass. My handwriting straggles as the dust makes the outlines of the paper invisible.

If I allow myself to sleep shall I ever awaken?

The rain has turned to snow and is falling in big soft flakes. Because of it the whole pace of the day has changed, for the rain came swiftly in lances blown by a sharp wind but the wind has dropped now and the snow drifts down almost dreamily. Gradually the garden is being covered and on the west front of the cathedral the new-carved saints wear white caps and the angels' wings are feathered with white like seagulls. When I came home that was the first thing I noticed, that great screen stripped of its scaffolding and made as clean and glorious as it was seven hundred years ago.

Spinny has begun making a snowman which Gran says she is too old for, but I don't know – why not? What has age to do with it? I have been out today and not for the first time. I am sure I could walk a mile and shall do when the weather gets better. For one thing, I weigh nearly what I ought to for a girl of my height and have only three more pounds to put on. This morning I walked as far as the university and stood outside the gates of St Leofric's Hall where I would have gone last October but for my illness. A student came up on a bicycle and passed in under the great stone arch. He smiled at me and said 'Hi!' and I smiled back, though saying nothing. But it was a great advance.

St Leofric's are keeping my place for me and I shall go there this coming autumn. By then I shall be over nineteen but what does that matter? I was so ill for so long after Luke died that I seem to have lost a piece out of my life, a vital area of my youth I shall never have back again. For, yes, Luke is dead and of the manner of his death I may be able to write one day but not now, certainly not now.... It is enough that I am able to confront it and think about it calmly.

I have changed a lot. I know I have, I feel it, but if my own ideas about myself are not enough, others keep telling me so. Gran, for one. After Luke died she shut up her own house and moved in here to live with us, to look after Spinny and be here to nurse me when I came out of hospital.

'You're a different girl, Elvira,' she said to me when, sitting up in bed and taking my supper tray from her, I used the childhood name we had for her.

'Gran.'

'I never said anything,' she said, 'but I watched you and listened to you and wondered how long it would be before you grew out of it, or if you ever would.'

'You hear of people having a mid-life-crisis,' I said. 'I went through an early life crisis, pre-life perhaps, because I haven't really started to live yet, have I?

'I was ordinary enough once,' I said, 'and then I seemed to go peculiar.'

'You had enough to make you peculiar, dear.'

She was thinking of Luke's death, remembering no doubt how I found him and what I saw.

'No, it was before that. It started when I was fourteen, it started with Mother's illness.'

And that same evening I hunted out the accounts I wrote of our life here after Mother died and when Mary Leonard came and what happened to us all. I blush for what I wrote then, for the kind of person I was. That affected, pedantic, arrogant, almost insane girl – was she really me? And for what imaginary reader was I creating all those false impressions?

The truest fact I noted about myself – though I played this down – was my fondness for Gothic novels and stories. Fondness is the wrong word and 'passion' would be nearer reality. I began to see myself as one of Poe's sickly heroines living in a house of doom, whereas the truth is I was no more than a neurotic teenager with a poor lonely puzzled little sister and a father who couldn't cope with being a widower and a parent. Poor Luke. I can see him more clearly now and understand him, assessing him as what he was, I am afraid; self-absorbed and uncaring, able to relate to us only as a teacher to his pupils. And here was an area where I drew the falsest picture of myself. For instance, although it's true that both Spinny and I learned Latin and Greek with Luke, I wasn't anywhere near as proficient as I've suggested. Nor was I up to teaching Spinny or reading *Antigone* at fifteen.

It is, I hope, a more honest diary that I'm embarking

on now. I've started it as much as anything for something to do during the coming year – the coming *sabbatical* year, if you can have a sabbatical without study to precede it – but I don't expect to write in it every day, for I have a lot of reading to do. Far from sailing through my A levels as I predicted I would in my supercilious way, I scarcely got grades high enough to satisfy the university and feel that if I had not been my father's daughter....

Gran hinted to me yesterday that an excess of humility on my part would be almost as bad as my former pride.

'You mustn't be a pendulum, darling,' she said, 'Always swinging this way and that.'

So I must be careful about that too. I must be altogether careful. The effect of those early life crisis years still shows in my prose, in pedantry and old-fashioned constructions. I shall be at pains to eradicate them. And this I must do before October when I shall begin writing essays for a tutor or supervisor.

The snow is falling heavily now and Spinny has completed her snowman just in time and set on its head an old black clerical hat that was probably our grandfather's. A sudden thick flurry has sent her running into the house. Five minutes and she will be in here with me. She is so pleased to have me home again and I know that much of my loneliness in hospital was due to missing her, not Luke.

In that past shameful time was I truly so discourteous to poor Mrs Cyprian? I simply can't remember, but if I was no one could have risen above it more than she or been greater-hearted, for she took everything into her hands that night, that early morning, those small hours, when Luke was dead and Spinny and I alone, orphans in this haunted house. (I must, I *will*, stop writing like that, but I'll leave the sentence as a warning to me.) Poor Mrs Cyprian! Imagine being wakened and fetched out of bed at three in the morning to find two shivering girls on your doorstep, one of them with bloody hands! She put on her coat and came back with us and saw to everything. And everything included seeing to *me*, getting an ambulance to take *me* to hospital, for the moment we came back into the hall I collapsed and lay on the floor unconscious.

I see it now as nature's way of saving me. But for that collapse, oblivion, long phase of semiconsciousness that followed, I certainly might have deluded myself about Luke's death. Just as there were times when I believed myself responsible for Mary Leonard's fall from the west front of the cathedral, so my psyche might have deceived me into thinking I had a hand in my father's dying. But from that I was saved. *That* was indisputable suicide, 'while the balance of his mind was disturbed', as Spinny afterwards told me the coroner had said.

Of course his death has benefited me not at all, unless one regards my inheritance as a benefit. Some would, no doubt. There is quite a lot of money and the house for Spinny and myself, Spinny's share to be held in trust until she is eighteen. The trustees are Gran and Luke's brother, our uncle Sebastian. They are all in favour of our moving out of here and can't understand why I want to stay. Poor Gran wants to go home and would be happy to take us with her.

'You can go and leave us,' I said to her yesterday. 'We

shall be all right on our own with Rosemary coming in twice a week. I'm over eighteen and lots of girls are married by my age.'

'I couldn't leave you alone with Spinny, darling,' she said.

What does she mean? I sometimes think she suspects me, that she remembers what I was, the way I used to be, and feels I am not to be trusted. Does she think I would starve Spinny, for instance? Or is it a general immaturity, a lack of responsibility in me, that she is afraid of?

'We could manage very well,' I said. 'Spinny is a good cook you know. Did you know? Luke would never let her do home economics at school but now he's – well, she's brilliant at it. She cooked supper the other night when Sheila had her evening off.'

Gran looked at me very tenderly. 'I know, dear. It does my heart good to see you eat. You don't know how worried about you I was when you were anorexic.'

I am pleased with myself. I resisted correcting her, I resisted telling her that strictly the word should be 'anorectic'. I am progressing.

While I was ill they cut off my hair. This always seems to be done to bedbound people, especially people who are comatose or semiconscious. Isn't it a strange thing that when Samson's hair was cut off it took his strength with it but the idea of cutting people's hair off today is so that their strength shouldn't be depleted? I wear my hair very short now and with a fringe, and sometimes I put make-up on my eyes.

'You'll be going out with boys next,' Spinny said to me today and perhaps she isn't far wrong.

At any rate I should like to and if I don't it's because I don't know any boys who might ask me. Except the student who smiled and said 'Hi!'. I dreamed of him last night. I dreamed that we were both on bicycles, cycling along in the countryside side by side, and I was very happy in the excited sort of way one can be when the horizon ahead is blue and mysterious and one wonders what lies over the next hill.

It is three days since I have written anything in this diary because I have been out so much and done so much. Gran and I went to London and bought me some clothes. We had lunch with Uncle Sebastian in a restaurant near his office and then we went to a matinée and got back here quite late – or late for me who has been used to being in bed by nine. The next day I should normally have rested but I didn't feel tired and I did what I had been meaning to do for weeks, months. I went into Luke's study for the first time and sat at his desk and looked at his handwriting and his books and finally opened the drawers of his desk. Something struck me forcibly and at first I felt disloyal, but then I thought, why not? Why shouldn't I feel like this? It's all right for me to feel like this. What I felt was (for the room has not been touched since Luke's death and only our solicitor and the valuer have been in there) how obsessively tidy Luke was, how orderly and meticulous, in almost a cold way. But I am still going to postpone writing about Luke.

The drawer in which Luke had kept his suicide letter I could not bring myself to open, though I knew of course that the note was no longer there. I could only touch the handle and withdraw my hand. In the drawer below were all the school reports for Spinny and me that had ever come to him, including the last two, received at the end of the spring term nearly a year ago.

I tried not to think about them. After all, they were a

year old. I closed the drawer and looked at Luke's books, arranged according to his own unique system and catalogued by him. For a moment I held Newman's *Apologia* against my cheek, my eyes shut. But I had to open that drawer again and read those reports again. The words that had been written about us made me wince: 'indifferent', 'lazy', 'self-absorbed' (me); 'backward', 'unable to concentrate' (Spinny).

She suffered more than I ever realised from the death of our mother. Luke and I should have made it up to her, but we didn't. We preferred each other's company. Or am I deluding myself there too and did Luke merely see another pupil in me, an exceptionally meek and obedient one? Still, it was for the best that Luke refused Spinny's request to be sent to boarding school and I am sure she felt this too – in her heart. I am glad she has Tom, even if they do behave like little kids together. What they like to do best is watch the Saturday morning continuous cartoon programme on Gran's televison. And they buy those sweets called Kinder, chocolate eggs with toys inside, that are aimed at the under-seven market.

The incongruous thing is that Spinny looks very unlike a little girl. She looks older than I, everyone says so, for she is tall and big, even overweight (all those Kinder), with wide hips and breasts like a woman of forty. Her skin is ripe peach colour with a dark downiness on her upper lip and her bright brown hair is a luxuriant bush. Our features are alike, I suppose, but otherwise we don't resemble each other. To look at her, if you didn't know her, you would think her serene, happy, smug even, insensitive, lacking in imagination, and guess her a sound sleeper. Only Gran and I know this is not so, for I am sure Tom has no idea what sort of nights she passes and what things she cries out.

The Cyprians' cat is dead. It wasn't run over but simply died of old age, I think, for they found its body stiff and cold in a dark corner of the coat cupboard. Nevertheless, Spinny still sees a cat in her bedroom most nights. Not directly, she says, not as you might see a real cat, sitting on a cushion opposite you and washing its whiskers, but out of the corner of her eye, on the periphery of vision, a cat that sneaks across the edge of her retina or is no more than a swift dark movement, a feline floater on her sideways glance. That is, for most of the time. But there are occasions, all too numerous, when the cat places itself in front of her and sitting on her bed, or on *her*, fixes its yellow unblinking eyes on her frightened brown ones – and it is then that she cries for help.

Of course when Gran and I come running there is never anything there. There is nothing there any more for Spinny either – but the smell of it. She can smell the cat, she says, even in its absence. All I can smell is the sweat of fear on Spinny's body.

'If we could find it,' she said the night before last, 'we could dig it out and throw it away.'

After we had left the room and closed the door Gran asked me what she meant.

'I suppose if we were to move . . . ?'

'You can't run away from a delusion,' Gran said. 'Whatever she sees is in her mind.'

I mentioned Dr Trewynne.

'I sometimes think,' Gran said, 'that a lot of Spinny's problems may be due to the drugs your Dr Trewynne has been plying her with for years.'

I love this house and don't want to leave it, in spite of

all the dreadful things that have happened here. I love the lane where you walk on hearts of stone and the walls hung with climbing roses, the cathedral's west front that is like a huge picture in relief on which there is always something new to find, to see. In those last months of his life poor Luke couldn't bear to look at it, put the light on in his study and kept the curtains drawn so that he should not see it. And when I put red dahlias in a vase for him he threw them away, saying the scarlet flowers reminded him of Mary Leonard lying dead on the hearts in her red dress.

After Spinny had gone to school I returned to the study. I sat with my eyes closed and my hands pressed against the cool grainy surface of the oak. After a moment or two I got up and went out into the garden and picked a handful of winter flowers, all that I could find among the patches of half-melted snow, a few snowdrops, a Christmas rose. These sad flowers I arranged in a vase and put them on the window-sill, keeping back one single snowdrop to lay beside my left hand. Then I took from the third drawer the first four chapters, all that he had completed, of 'Noogenesis'. I sat there looking at it, and not looking, the words incomprehensible, a dancing meaningless mass.

If I had been able to foresee, a year ago, that Luke would die like this, I am sure I would have vowed to myself to finish this work of his at all costs, even if I had to acquire a theology degree to do it. Now this seemed absurd. I could never do it, nor would I wish to. But instead of disloyalty or guilt, a kind of joy filled my mind that I hadn't sacrificed all my youth, my very life perhaps, to misplaced learning and self-absorption. In the very nick of time I had been saved from it, pulled back from the edge, delivered through a long catharsis into normality.

It was, of course, Luke's death that had saved me.

Now I can write of it. I can re-live that summer night when I was myself on the brink of dissolution. They told me that if I had gone on much longer with the life I had been living, I should first have lost my sight, then there would have been kidney failure. They told me other things too. The golden down that grew all over my body is a manifestation of anorexia. I saw it only as some kind of sign of my super-humanity, almost akin to stigmata. That night I lay on the spread blanket on the grass, looking in the last of the light at the gleaming fur on my skeletal arms and feeling the same fluffy down on my concave stomach, my breastless chest.

The sky had become a jewel-like dark blue with a burning rim of sunset on the horizon. The white philadelphus Gran calls orange blossom filled the air with a scent that was sickly, overcoming the lighter, sharper, perfume of our red roses. I lay looking up at Luke's closed window, waiting for the light to go out and for Luke to come and open the casement. The way I foresaw this happening was that we wouldn't speak but acknowledge each other only by a long gaze, a tender and adoring meeting of our eyes, and after this, I felt, I should die in peace.

How ignorant I was about the form death takes and how it comes! I supposed death from starvation would be a painless slipping away, having no notion then of blindness due to vitamin depletion, of scurvy and anaemia and fluid retention and collapse. Poe didn't know much about dying either and he and his fellows taught me wrong.

It was strange too that I deceived myself about this closeness with Luke, for we had not been close for a long time, but estranged, remote from each other, even hostile. If, then, I had been capable of honesty with myself, I would have confessed to a feeling for him closer to hatred than to love.

It had become too dark for me to continue reading my Poe. With my eyes fixed on Luke's window, that golden rectangle, I fell asleep. Or this is how, for a long while, I like to think of myself falling asleep. The truth, no doubt, is that I buried my head in my arms and lay on my stomach.

It was Spinny who awakened me. I opened my eyes and in the moonlight saw her standing over me with the blank face and dull eyes of a sleepwalker. I don't believe I ever asked her why she had got up, what had made her look for me, and when I wasn't to be found, for Luke. Perhaps I took it for granted, even then, that she had seen or heard one of her ghosts.

'There's something you must see,' she said.

I asked her what she meant.

'Something on the carpet. I can't have imagined it, can I? I did look carefully. I put the light on and looked again and I looked away and looked again. I can't have *dreamed* it. And his light's still on.'

I was cold, from the dew and the night, but from dread too.

'I shouted out,' said Spinny, 'but he didn't answer.'

His light was still on, a multitude of moths swarming and fluttering against the bright panes.

I was weak. I don't really know where I got the strength to walk into the house and climb the stairs. At some point, I remember, I held on to Spinny's arm. In the passage outside Luke's door, just underneath the door itself where the carpet started – Luke's austere room had a floor of bare boards like an anchorite's cell – a red stain had seeped through the pale wool fibres. We looked at each other, Spinny and I, and her face was like stone, specifically like marble, from which all colour has been bleached.

She said to me, 'You're as white as a ghost.'

Spinny opened the door. It kills me to write of it, even now, seven months afterwards. There was so much blood, a river of it, not yet fully congealed, that had flowed from the bed and across the floor as if to announce (as it had done) what lay inside. He was on his back, dressed but with his shirt open at the neck and the sleeves rolled up, and he was whiter than either of us, a bloodless waxen white, for all his blood had flowed out through those cut arteries in his wrists.

The cut-throat razor which had been our grandfather's, pearl-handled, unused for years, housed in its hide case, lay on the pillow beside his head, and on the other pillow, carefully placed there, weighted down with a piece of stone from the Parthenon some ancestor had brought back before this was a crime, was the letter he had written to me. For ultimate use, I now saw. He hadn't changed his mind. This was what he had always intended.

I write coolly. I wasn't cool then. We both burst into screams at the sight. Why I touched him I don't know, perhaps to see if his life might even then be saved, to feel the temperature of him. The hideous spectacle of my red hands set Spinny screaming more loudly, running to the window and opening it at last, howling to the night. No one heard her, no one came. We stumbled down the stairs, out of the house, running we didn't know where, looking for help from any source, finding ourselves on Mrs Cyprian's doorstep, sobbing and crying as we pounded on the knocker, hammered at the bell and kneeling on the stone step, called for help through the letterbox.

That was Luke's death; that was what happened. Almost immediately I collapsed and became seriously ill. They took me away to hospital but I have no memory of that, no recollection of anything that followed for weeks and weeks, until I awoke one morning to find my hair all gone, and the down gone from my body too, and Gran sitting there, preparing to tell me I hadn't dreamed it; she gave it to me as they had cut it off, two golden braids secured with elastic bands and sealed up in a freezer bag.

Very gently and gradually, over the weeks that followed, she told me of the aftermath of Luke's death, of the inquest and the suicide verdict. Luke had drugged himself before he did it, washing down sedatives with his bedtime drink. It consoled Gran a little, I think, as it consoled me, to know that he must have been on the point of sleep, on the very brink of oblivion, when he used the razor....

The house seemed dream-like, unreal, when I returned to it. It looked the same but the core of it, the spirit maybe, was missing. Two days later Gran gave me the key to Luke's study and she gave me the letter Luke wrote to me, which the coroner returned when he had done with it. But it has taken me a long time to come in, to use the key as well as break the invisible, intangible seals that closed off the study. Yesterday, on my second visit, I noticed how thickly the dust lies. There is something sinister and strange about a room which is both exquisitely tidy and covered with dust, as the tomb of some ancient king must surely be when the first archaeologists enter it.

Rosemary may as well be allowed in here now to clean the room and air it. There is something unhealthy about maintaining mausoleums. I said this to Spinny when, coming home from school, she tiptoed over the threshold of the study and stood there in silent awe.

I had been thinking of changes we might make. Luke's bedroom it might be as well to consider never using, but the study, untidied a bit, rearranged, I might keep for myself. Spontaneously, I offered Spinny two new rooms for herself, the best guest bedroom and communicating dressing room on the first floor. I say 'offered' and not 'suggested' because it is still for me to offer or withhold and will be for the next three years until she becomes eighteen. But I am determined not to abuse my power or even stress it and I spoke gently.

Her response was unexpected.

'No one ever saw a ghost in the guest room, did they?'

I said I was sure they hadn't. 'But no one's used our guest room except Uncle Sebastian years and years ago.'

She looked at me. 'And Mary Leonard,' she said, and there was a note of incredulity. 'You hadn't forgotten Mary Leonard?'

I had for a moment. Had she in fact made little impression on me or am I doing what is called 'blocking' her off? Spinny came up to me and put her arms round my neck. She does this sometimes, very warmly and sweetly, and I wish I could be more responsive, I wish I liked physical contact more. She gave a little laugh.

'You won't look through the floor at me?'

'Would I?'

'I don't know. I can never be sure what you'll do.' But she was still smiling, her eyes bright, as if those bad nights never happened.

'I'll move into that room,' she said. 'But I'd rather we moved house. Can't we?'

I said I would think about it. I love this house, though. I shall never leave it.

I have spoken to my student; I talked to him and we are going to the cinema together. It is like a miracle and I can still hardly believe it. His name is Daniel and he is in his second year at the university where he is reading philosophy and political economy. I met him in Carey's where I was waiting for Spinny after she came out of school.

These days I eat. I eat quite a lot, though not the sticky confections of marzipan and chocolate and whipped cream Spinny is so fond of. Isn't she lucky that she never gets a spot but her skin is always clear and glowing? Carey's is one of those places which have a window onto the street full of marvellous-looking delectable gateaux and pastries while at the back of the shop is an area where one can sit and 'stuff oneself', as Spinny puts it. I had been sitting there about ten minutes and the place was filling up with students. I know now that I was looking for Daniel, though I wouldn't have admitted this even to myself at the time.

Spinny was late, as she often is, and after a while I got up, leaving my coat on one of the chairs and went to fetch myself an espresso and a Harvest Crunch bar from the counter. Coming back to the table, I found Daniel sitting on the other chair, unwinding from his neck the long striped university scarf he always wears even on quite mild spring days like this one. Of course I didn't know his name then and I didn't quite know what to say.

He said it for me. He jumped up and apologised. He hadn't known this seat was taken. I said I was waiting for my sister but there were three chairs anyway. And then I plucked up courage and said we'd met before, outside St Leofric's gates.

'Of course,' he said. 'It *was* you. I've been trying to think how I knew your face, and do you know, I thought I'd dreamt you? I'm always seeing wonderful faces in dreams but they hardly ever turn out to be real people.'

Which was a very good beginning.

We told each other our names and he said he was in his second year at St Leofric's and I said I would be going there in October. I told him I was an orphan and he said he was too, his parents having been killed in a car crash. He told me how he always wore this scarf, how he is famous for it, everyone knows him by his scarf which is three metres long. It was nice because he remembered Luke, had been at one of his lectures and said he could see I was his daughter. And then he said he liked the way I talk because it sounds old-fashioned and precise and like nothing he had heard before, only read of.

Spinny came at last and Tom with her and that gave me a very strange feeling, the four of us sitting there together, talking and drinking coffee. It made me feel like a *young girl* for the first time ever almost, an ordinary young girl doing what other young girls do. It must have shown in my face, for my sister, eating a chocolate éclair, looked at me and smiled.

Yet since then she has awakened me two nights running with her screams. Moving into the guest room has made no difference, it seems. When I rushed in the place was ablaze with light and I saw that Spinny had replaced the bulb in the hanging lamp with one of much higher wattage. As well as her bedlamp she had two table lamps, one of which she must have brought from Luke's room, the other from downstairs. She was standing by the bed, trembling.

'Green Margery came in and spoke my name. She said, Despina, Despina.'

'*Who* came in?' I said.

'The witch woman,' Spinny said. 'The witch woman whose cat they buried in the wall. Don't you remember?'

I did then, of course. I remembered the story Luke told us. Spinny clung to me and I forced myself not to show the revulsion I felt at the sweetish smell that hangs about her, a smell like acetone and boiled sugar. On the following night it was the cat itself that came. It sat on her, she said, and woke her by touching her face with its paw. Spinny had kept a light on, so that she was able to see the cat quite clearly and see the dust on it, dust and bits of plaster and cobwebs as if it had been inside a wall.

Only a week has passed but in it everything has changed – for better and for worse. Daniel and I have met three times and that has been good. I couldn't begin to record our conversations though, we've talked so much and

about all things under the sun. We really like each other
– and more than that.

Another good thing was that a man Gran met asked
her if our house would come up for sale. An estate agent
told him it was worth what seems to me an enormous
sum of money but he said he was willing to pay this. Of
course I refused even to think of it but it is nice to know
one's home is so highly valued. After that the bad things
came thick and fast.

Uncle Sebastian is ill. He has had to go into hospital for
an emergency operation. We hardly know him, I
suppose we have met him no more than nine or ten times
in our whole lives, but he is Gran's only surviving child
and she is desperately worried, terrified when the phone
rings, yet longing to hear. The other thing that has
happened is simply bizarre. All over the house on the
ground floor holes keep appearing in the walls. They are
like the holes an electrician makes to put a new electric
point in, about six inches square but irregular, showing
the laths within and the crumbly plaster between them.
In places though the laths themselves have been cut or
apparently hammered in and then there are great gaping
fissures, dark inside and empty or else containing a
jumble of torn paper and wood shavings and the
everlasting spiders' webs. I wonder if this could be the
effect of some kind of dry rot that perhaps takes place in
old houses when they reach a certain age, rather like
metal fatigue in aircraft. Two nights ago I counted five
such holes, two in the drawing room, one in the hall, one
in the passage and one in the dining room. I unlocked the
door to Luke's study – I keep the key myself – but there
were none in there. Next morning, though, another had

appeared in the drawing room, in the right-hand corner of the fireplace. I phoned the builder who does odd jobs for us and he said he would come as soon as he could, whenever that will be.

Gran is too worried to care. She paces up and down, looking at her watch and then at the phone, one hand to her lips as if to stop herself from crying out. At teatime she was so preoccupied that for once she neglected to stop Spinny overeating and my greedy little sister devoured nearly a whole Battenburg cake before Gran reached out a languid hand to slide the plate away.

That was yesterday, Thursday. In the evening Daniel took me to a disco. I was dreading it, I thought I should hate it, it seemed the antithesis of everything I liked and admired and wanted to do but the funny thing is, I *loved* it, it was amazing. I would have liked to stay there dancing all night and I only made Daniel take me away because I thought Gran might be anxious, and she has anxieties enough at the moment.

He brought me home and we came into the house together and I showed him the holes in the walls. Two more had appeared in the hall while I was out. Not dry rot definitely, Daniel said, but made perhaps by some animal. Why did that make me think of the cat, for cats never dig holes, do they?

He has to go home for the weekend but we have arranged to meet on Monday, 'I'm really going to miss you,' he said, and I felt so happy. I waved to him and watched him walk off down the lane in the moonlight, his shadow very long on the hearts of stone, the shadow of the two ends of his scarf floating from his back like wings. I want to be nice for him, I want to be *good*. Not when I am with him but when we have just parted the past comes back to me and I ask myself if I killed Luke and Mary Leonard.

Perhaps I did – but, oh, I hope I did not! It is true that I can't remember, but there are two things which militate against my guilt, which reassure me. One is that I never in my life possessed a penknife or carried one about with me and the other is that when Luke died I was half-way to death myself; I lacked the strength to cut the arteries in a man's wrists.

Suddenly tiredness overwhelmed me like an iron weight pressing on my head. Only a few weeks ago I was still in hospital, scarcely able to get out of bed. The way I dragged myself upstairs reminded me of the night Luke died, when I crawled, clinging to Spinny. When I reached my bedroom I took out Woodhouse's English Greek Dictionary and there, behind it, was the jar containing cyanide. Why have I kept it so long? Partly, I think – I truly think this – I've kept it because it is hard to know how to dispose of it. Now, of course, I must throw it away as soon as I have the opportunity.

In spite of being so tired, I slept badly. I don't think I slept at all until about five and when I awoke it was still quite dark from the thick mist that pressed against the windows. The mist disappeared around lunchtime and it has been clear ever since, the sun shining and the sky blue. Gran is happy because when she phoned the hospital they told her Uncle Sebastian was better and had had a comfortable night. She wants to go up to London and see him; she could go tomorrow and be back on Sunday night, but she doesn't like to leave me alone, she says. I have told her Spinny and I will be perfectly all right and reassured her as best I can and I think she means to go, for she has gone off to the kitchen to cook us a chicken for tomorrow's lunch and bake a cake.

I am going to try and sleep for a while.

Something curious has happened. The cyanide has disappeared. I took out all the dictionaries to make sure and there is no doubt the jar has gone. The probable answer is that Rosemary took it and threw it out when she cleaned the room yesterday, for it is obvious the dictionaries have all been dusted. I remember her doing something like that once before. Not throwing out cyanide, of course, but a nearly full jar of peppermint rock she found in Spinny's room. I shall have to ask Rosemary about it when she comes on Monday; it is too much of a risk not to, as cyanide is about the most lethal substance known.

I suppose I have written this down first to avoid confronting something worse because, though it could be serious enough, it is not the most disquieting thing that has happened. Yet I did worry about it all the morning, I wondered what I should do, if there was anything I could do before Monday. Spinny and Tom sat in Gran's room watching the cartoons on her television, eating sweets and giggling. They had to have the light on, we put lights on all over the house, for the fog was thicker than yesterday. When first I got up the west front of the cathedral was invisible, a dense grey blanket hanging between it and our windows. After a while the sun came through and for a time I could see the saints and apostles and six-winged seraphim gleaming through the mist in an other-worldly way or as if they were alive and truly transported to live among the clouds. Then, by noon, the fog closed in and hung thick and stifling against our small mullioned panes.

It was after that when I first went into the kitchen. I hadn't felt like eating breakfast. The first thing I saw was another great hole in the wall, just above the wainscot. On the floor beneath lay a heap of plaster crumbs and horsehair. I felt a sudden desire to be out of the house, to go somewhere for the day and perhaps the coming night too, but where could I go in this fog? And who with? Daniel is away. Gran has gone to London. Spinny went with Tom when he left, walking along beside his bicycle in search of chips and hamburgers. I ate my lunch alone. Afterwards I went into Luke's study and sat there reading Newman, as he always did when he was worried or unhappy.

I must have fallen asleep over the book – it is too soon for me to go disco-dancing. I should have known better but later on, about five, the sounds of hammering and scraping woke me up. I thought the builder must have come and Spinny let him in. There was no need for me to see him – what use would I be? But I did go out there. I wanted a drink of water, and it wasn't the builder but my little sister crouching on the floor and digging into the wall with a hammer and chisel for all she was worth.

It was strange really, I didn't ask her what she was doing. I knew. I knew what she was looking for. For a long time I didn't think of anything much but just did routine things, went into the kitchen, poured myself a glass of water, ate an apple, opened the fridge and looked at the pie Gran had left us for our supper, sat at the table and read the paper which Spinny must have brought in and left there unopened.

At about seven or a bit later we sat down together and

ate the pie. It was dark outside, not a star showing, the moon hidden behind a mile of fog. It *is* dark, it is like that now, and as silent as in the old days before Mary Leonard brought her record player and Gran her television. Somehow I haven't felt like having either on. I have been thinking about Spinny and about the penknife she got in her Christmas stocking the last Christmas before Mother died, about how she too was on the scaffolding and she too knew of Luke's letter to me. I watched her while we were eating supper. Can you have the opposite of anorexia? If you can, Spinny has it. I noticed tonight how enormously she eats: three-quarters of a veal and ham pie big enough for six people, half a loaf of bread, the slices thickly spread with butter, a litre-size of raspberry ripple ice-cream.

She is bursting out of her clothes. The label on her blouse was turned up out of the neck and when she turned her back (to reach for the bag of marshmallows) I saw it was a size eighteen. But it will soon be too small for her. Her hair is as long as mine used to be but dark and curly and bushlike. Her round, triple-chinned face glistens with a kind of adolescent bloom and her cheeks are as red as the ice-cream she has just eaten.

She is going to make us a cup of coffee. I have been sitting in Luke's study writing all this down quite quickly, I don't know why. No coffee has yet appeared, though Spinny has been in once and dismayed me further by showing me the skeleton of a bird's wing, unmistakably a bird's wing with a pathetic feather still clinging to it along with the plaster dust.

'Could these be the cat's bones, Elvira?' she said very quietly and wistfully, such a small voice to come from a big girl's full lips.

'I don't think so, darling,' I said gently.

'I'd like to find the bones and make it go,' she said. 'But when I've left this house and moved it won't matter, will it?'

What does she mean? She hardly knows herself. But I know. I think I know everything and I am filled with pity and terror. So much is going to happen on Monday, let us just get through tonight and Sunday, let us just get through. Tomorrow night Gran will be back. On Monday I shall ask Rosemary about the missing jar, I shall make Dr Trewynne get Spinny to a psychiatrist, I shall see Daniel. There is only a short time to get through, no more than twenty-four hours, and I will be very kind to her during those hours, very gentle, I will do everything she asks of me.

I can hear her coming now with my coffee. To please her and make her easy I shall drink it, every drop. We shall sit together quietly and I shall write no more....